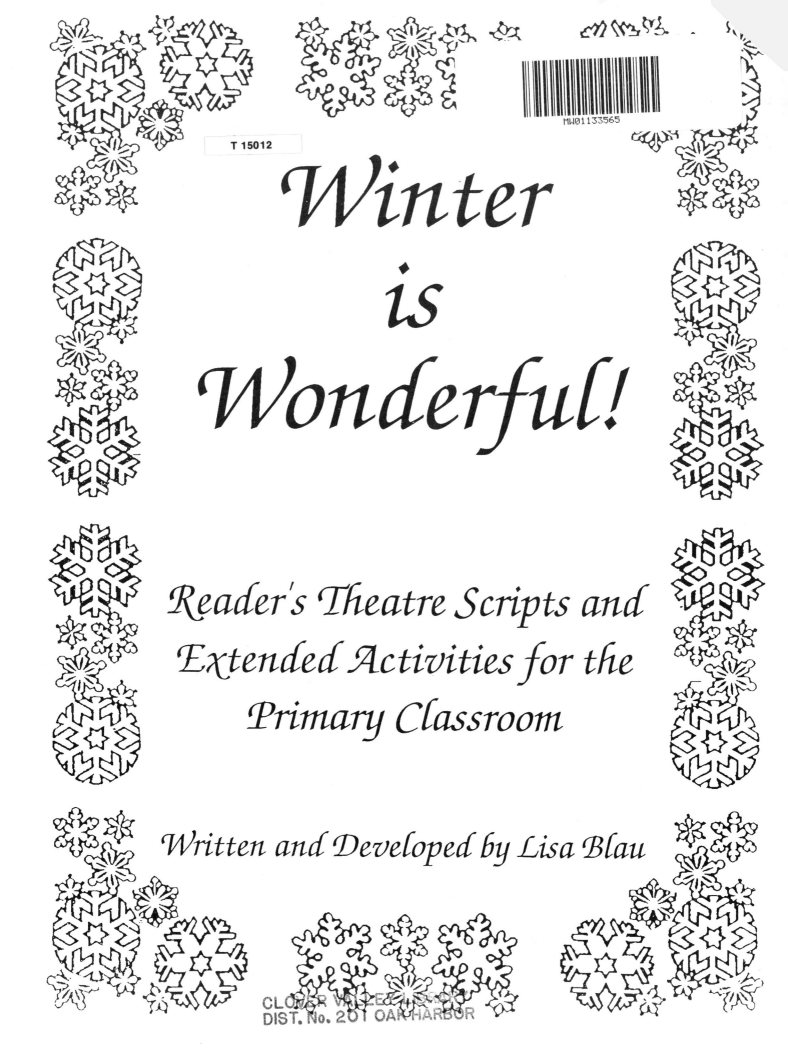

Winter is Wonderful!

Reader's Theatre Scripts and Extended Activities for the Primary Classroom

Written and Developed by Lisa Blau

Copyright © 1994
One From the Heart
Educational Resources

All Rights Reserved
Printed in the United States of America
Published by One From the Heart Educational Resources
14150 NE 20th Street • Suite #223
Bellevue, WA 98007

ISBN 0-9640333-2-1

Table of Contents

 *Winter Is Wonderful!*

Dear Readers,

   BRRR! When winter's chill fills the air and those rainy day blues start to take over...QUICK!!!...reach for this book! The exciting scripts and extended activities are sure to spark your students' curiosity and interest. Extended activities for science, poetry writing and even a super-sweet play about Valentine's Day are all part of this terrific resource book.

   Reader's Theatre scripts are exciting to use because they can be used in every part of the curriculum and most importantly...students LOVE them! These scripts have been performed many times in my classroom and much of the artwork you see was created by my students.

I am indeed proud of their help in making this book become a reality. I dedicate this book to my students...they are my inspiration.

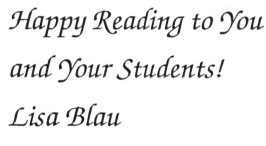

Happy Reading to You
and Your Students!
Lisa Blau

Helpful Hints

♥ The best advice I can give to those of you who have not tried Reader's Theatre is to simply jump right in and get started! There are no rules with Reader's Theatre, it is an open and flowing activity guaranteed to get your students truly excited about reading. Here are a few ideas that may help you along the way:

♥ It's easiest to begin with a shorter script. The best place to start is with a piece of poetry. Two different poems appear in this book and I would suggest using, "The Snowflake Dance" first. It's short, it's sweet and children will enjoy cutting out their own snowflakes from construction paper and copying the poem onto the snowflake.

♥ Poems work well in the beginning because you can easily model appropriate Reader's Theatre behavior. That is, readers must speak loudly, clearly, and with <u>LOTS</u> of enthusiasm. They must maintain eye-contact with the audience. Remind children to smile...Reader's Theatre afterall is great fun. I always say, "When you are wearing a smile, you are always dressed in style" just prior to our performance. Try it...it works!

♥   Be sure to run off enough scripts so that every student has an individual copy. Members of the listening audience can read along as their classmates perform the scripts. Rotate parts so that everyone has a chance to be a reader and a listener. That's the marvelous thing about using Reader's Theatre...everyone is <u>actively</u> engaged!

♥   Prior to reading our scripts, I ask the children to mark any unfamiliar words. We list these new words on the board and discuss each word's meaning by reading the word as it appears in the script. Any of your favorite pre-reading and vocabulary lessons can be adapted whenever you share a script with your students.

♥   If you are lucky enough to have some music stands, try using them. Students can place their scripts upon the music stands and pass the pages across the stand. This frees up their hands to add gestures and helps your student readers maintain greater eye-contact with their audiences. If you don't have music stands, use a long table for students to place their scripts upon...the long table will work just as nicely as the stands!

♥   Be sure to honor students' reading achievement by giving them one of the certificates at the back of this resource book.

The Snowflake Dance

A Reader's Theatre Script
Based upon a poem by Lisa Blau

Reader #1	Reader #2	Reader #3

Reader #1 -   Snowflakes dance

Reader #2 -   And snowflakes fly

Reader #3 -   Snowflakes twirl gently across the sky

Reader #1 -   No two are alike

Reader #2 -   Each one as unique as can be

All -   Snowflakes are a lot like you and me

The Mitten

An Old Folktale
A Reader's Theatre Script
Written and Developed by Lisa Blau

Narrator #1	Grandmother	Raccoon
Narrator #2	Mouse	Rabbit
Narrator #3	Flea	Bear
	Boy	Fox

Narrator #1 - Once upon a time a young boy lived in a small cottage with his grandmother.

Narrator #2 - The cottage was deep in the woods. During the winter, it snowed and snowed and a cold wind always blew hard.

Narrator #3 - The boy's grandmother made him a beautiful pair of mittens.

Grandmother - These mittens will keep your hands nice and warm. Now when you walk in the snow, you will not be cold.

Narrator #1 -	The grandmother told the boy.
Boy -	Oh, thank you, grandmother. These are the most beautiful mittens I have ever seen!
Narrator #3 -	The boy said to his grandmother.
Narrator #1 -	The next day the boy went to play in the snow. He caught snowflakes on his tongue and made a tall, fat snowman with black stone eyes.
Narrator #3 -	After a happy day full of play, the boy walked back to his cottage. Along the way he dropped one of his new mittens.
Narrator #1 -	Along came a tiny mouse. She was scurrying through the snow when she saw the boy's mitten.
Mouse -	I am cold as cold can be. What a warm little house this will make for me. I shall live here most happily.
Narrator #1 -	Said the little mouse. And the little mouse climbed into the mitten.

Narrator #2 -	By and by a raccoon came running along. He saw the mitten and said...
Raccoon -	I am as cold as cold can be. What a warm little house this will make for me. I shall live here most happily.
Mouse -	Come in, my friend.
Narrator #3 -	The little mouse said to the raccoon.
Narrator #2 -	So the raccoon climbed into the mitten with the mouse.
Narrator #1 -	By and by a rabbit came hopping along. He saw the mitten and said...
Rabbit -	I am as cold as cold can be. What a warm little house this will make for me. I shall live here most happily.
Mouse -	Come in my friend.
Raccoon -	Yes, we have room for you.
Narrator #3 -	The mouse and the raccoon said to the rabbit.
Narrator #1 -	So the rabbit climbed into the mitten with the mouse and the raccoon.

Narrator #2 -	By and by a fox came running by. He saw the mitten and said...
Fox -	I am as cold as cold can be. What a warm little house this will make for me. I shall live here most happily.
Mouse -	Come in, my friend.
Raccoon -	Yes, we have room for you.
Rabbit -	Come and join us.
Narrator #3 -	The mouse, raccoon, and rabbit said to the fox.
Narrator #2 -	So the fox climbed into the mitten with the mouse, the raccoon and the rabbit.
Narrator #1 -	By and by a bear came running by. The bear saw the mitten and said...
Bear -	I am as cold as cold can be. What a warm little house this will make for me. I shall live here most happily.
Mouse -	Wait! You are too big!

Raccoon -	Yes! We are crowded in the mitten already!
Fox -	There isn't any room for you, Mr. Bear.
Narrator #3 -	The mouse, raccoon, rabbit and fox said to the bear.
Narrator #1 -	But the bear did not listen. He pushed his way into the crowded little mitten. The seams of the mitten stretched and stretched.
Narrator #2 -	By and by a tiny flea came along.
Mouse -	Wait! You cannot fit in here!
Raccoon -	Yes, we are crowded in here already!
Rabbit -	Please do not come in!
Fox -	There isn't room for you, Mr. Flea.
Bear -	My friends are right, this mitten is stretched tight.
Flea -	Nonsense! There's room for me...I am very tiny as you can see.

Narrator #1 -   The flea said to the animals.

Narrator #2 -   Then the flea hopped into the mitten.

Narrator #3 -   Suddenly the mitten was stretched too far...much too far.

Narrator #1 -   The animals were so very crowded together that the little flea sneezed.

Flea (loudly) -   Ah...Ah...Ah...Ah...Ah...CHOO!

Narrator #3 -   What a loud sneeze from such a tiny creature!

Narrator #1 -   That mighty sneeze sent the mitten and all of the animals flying through the snow.

Narrator #2 -   The mitten flew through the air and landed on the front steps of the boy's cottage.

Boy -   What is this? My lost mitten! How did it get here?

Narrator #3 -   The boy said as he looked around the forest.

Boy -   Ah, well...no **need to** worry. I've got the mitten **with me.**

Narrator #1 -   And with that, **the boy** stepped into his warm little **cottage** and hugged his grandmother **tightly.**

All -   The End.

- Writing! Writing! Writing! Have children re-write the story in their own words in a mini-book shaped like a mitten. This is a <u>perfect</u> activity to share with upper-grade buddies.

- Mitten Math! Have students trace around their hands to form a mitten shape. (This is a <u>perfect</u> partner activity!) Have children estimate how many snowballs (mini marshmallows) will cover his/her mitten. Have children compare actual amount with estimate. You may wish to chart this information. (Use the attached worksheet for this super activity!)

- Learning to count by 2's?! Have children color pairs of mittens and post on a chart. As an extension, have students write number sentences based on the chart.
Note: To count by three's make snowmen for your chart!

- Make a "Mitten Math" classbook by having children write and illustrate math problems based on the chart. You can use 5x8 cards with the question on one side and the answer along with an illustration on the other side. Got an extra five minutes? Use the cards for a quick math drill!

Mitten Math

1. Trace around your hand to make the shape of a mitten.

2. Estimate how many snowballs will fit into your mitten.
    Write your guess here_____.

3. How many snowballs fit on your mitten? _____.
    Compare your answers.

♥ **Increase Your Brain Power!** Write two story problems about mittens on the back of this page. Ask a friend to solve your super stumpers! Have fun math stars!

Christmas Around The World

A Reader's Theatre Script
Written and Developed by Lisa Blau

Narrator #1	Felipe	Domenico
Narrator #2	Anita	Henrick
Narrator #3	Marta	Katrina
	Hans	Ingrid

Narrator #1 - Good morning! Welcome to our special program called, "Christmas Around the World."

Narrator #2 - Today you will learn how children in other countries celebrate Christmas.

Narrator #3 - We'll learn how Christmas is celebrated in Mexico, Italy, Sweden and Germany.

Narrator #1 - So sit back and relax. You'll travel around the world with us without even leaving your chair!

Felipe -

I live in Mexico. We open our gifts on January 6 instead of Christmas Day. We do not hang our stockings on the fireplace. We put our shoes out. The Wise Men will fill our shoes with toys and candy.

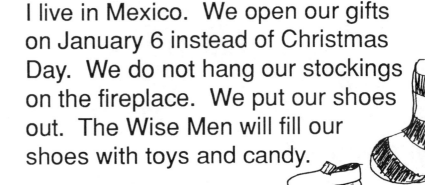

Anita -

Feliz Navidad! My name is Anita. I also live in Mexico. In our country, the children gather together to celebrate the "Posadas". We travel from house to house with lighted candles. It is my favorite part of the holidays.

Lucia -

Buon Natale! My name is Marta. I live in Italy. We sing Christmas carols and light candles on Christmas Eve as each child tells about the story of Christmas.

Domenico -

Buon Natale! My name is Domenico. I live in Italy. A nice old witch named La Befana brings children gifts on January 6. If we have been naughty, La Befana will leave us rocks, sticks, or pieces of coal instead of toys and candies.

Henrick -

Froehliche Weihnachten! My name is Henrick. I live in Germany. Our country was the first to use a Christmas tree. Long ago Christmas trees were lit with candles. In some families the mothers decorated the trees and the children got the first look at the beautifully decorated tree on Christmas morning.

Katrina -

Froehliche Weihnachten! My name is Katrina. I live in Germany. Some German children dress in masks and travel from house to house knocking on their neighbor's doors. The three Thursdays before Christmas are known as Knocking Nights. The children make loud noises to scare away any evil spirits.

Hans -

God Jul! My name is Hans. I live in Sweden. Swedish families celebrate St. Lucia Day on December 13. The oldest daughter wears a white robe, a red sash, and a crown of lighted candles on her head.

Ingrid -

God Jul! My name is Ingrid. I live in Sweden.

Early in the morning the oldest daughter will make sweet rolls to serve her family. Gifts are opened on Christmas Eve. The families will go to church on Christmas morning.

Narrator #1 -   Wow! We've learned so much about how people celebrate Christmas in other lands.

Narrator #2 -   Christmas is a happy time for everyone. A time for giving...a time for love.

Narrator #3 -   It's a time for sharing all that is special with our families and friends.

Narrator #1 -   So, from all of us, to all of you...

Felipe and Maria -   Feliz Navidad!

Lucia and Domenico - Buon Natale!

Henrick and Katrina - Froehliche Weihnachten!

Hans and Ingrid -   God Jul!

Narrators
#1, #2, #3 -   Merry Christmas!

- Prior to reading the script, ask students to describe some of the ways that they celebrate the holidays with their families. You may wish to have students write about a favorite holiday tradition in their families. You may wish to have students write about a favorite holiday tradition in their journals. If students so desire, they may read their journal entries to the class.

- Be sure to mark each reader's part with a highlighter pen for easier reading. If you would like to adapt this script for a holiday performance, costumes could be added quite easily and inexpensively. The children representing Mexico could wear serapes. The children from Italy could wear green and red clothing. The girl from Italy could wear a bandana on her head. The children from Sweden could wear white clothing. A wreath or paper candles could be worn by the girl reading the part of "Ingrid". The children from Germany could wear warm sweaters in Christmas colors. A background of holiday symbols from each country could also be painted by your students. The background could include a Christmas tree, a pinata, and a picture of La Befana, for example.

- Children will enjoy trying holiday foods from other countries. You may wish to have an "International Buffet" as part of your holiday celebration. Enlist the help of your Room Mothers to have parents send in a traditional recipe or two.

- It's always a nice idea to make a special remembrance that children can take home and share with their families. An easy ornament can be made by providing each child with a dessert-size red or green paper plate. Provide pieces of Christmas wrapping paper or old Christmas card pictures that have been cut out with pinking shears. Students can glue a "collage" of pictures onto their plates, then add a colorful piece of curling ribbon for hanging. These are colorful ornaments that kids love to make and best of all...you can teach students about recycling by using those scraps of gift wrap and last year's Christmas cards!

One final note - As our student populations change, some school districts are opting to omit the celebration of Christmas in the classroom. I think it is terribly important for teachers to be sensitive to our students' beliefs. Therefore, before sharing this unit with your students, ask yourself if there are any students in your class whose families do not celebrate Christmas. You may also wish to share information about Channukah or Kwanza with students so that they realize that not everyone celebrates Christmas. My goal is to teach students about traditions in other countries and focus on the love of family and the importance of giving during the holiday season. What are your goals?

Pronunciation Guide

Country/Language	Spelling	Pronunciation
Mexico (Spanish)	Feliz Navidad	Feh-leez Na-Vee-dahd
German	Froehliche Weihnachten	Fruh-lee-keh Vigh-nach-ten
Swedish	God Jul	Good Yewl
Italian	Buon Natale	Bwone Na-tah-leh

The Three Coins
An Old Tale of China

A Reader's Theatre Script
Written and Developed by Lisa Blau

Reader #1	Reader #4	Chang
Reader #2	Reader #5	The Old Man
Reader #3		

Reader #5 - Long ago a poor man named Chang sold rice for a living in China.

Reader #2 - Every day Chang walked up and down the narrow streets carrying two baskets of rice.

Reader #3 - Chang carried the baskets on the ends of a long bamboo pole. He also carried a gong tied with a bit of rope.

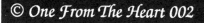

Reader #4 -   When Chang found a good place to stop, he would set down his two baskets, strike the gong and call out...

Chang -   Rice! Rice! I have rice for sale!

Reader #4 -   Now one day a funny looking man came up to Chang.

Reader #1 -   The old man had a long white beard and wore ragged clothes.

Reader #3 -   The old man spoke to Chang...

Old Man -   Young man, I should like to buy some rice. I will fill this one small bowl.

Chang -   Help yourself, Old Man.

Reader #2 -   Chang said to the Old Man.

Reader #5 -   Chang saw that the Old Man's rice bowl was very tiny, it would not hold much rice and besides...the Old Man did not look like he had any money.

Reader #3 -	Chang was always kind to those who were poor.
Reader #2 -	Chang watched as the Old Man piled handful after handful of rice into his tiny bowl.
Reader #3 -	The Old man emptied one of Chang's baskets, then the other.
Reader #4 -	Then the old man dropped three coins into one of Chang's empty baskets and walked away.
Chang -	I have been robbed! I have been robbed!
Reader #2 -	Wailed Chang as he stared at the empty baskets.
Reader #3 -	Yet Chang could not explain how the old man had taken all of the rice in his tiny, tiny bowl.
Chang -	Well, I shall go home now. I have no more rice to sell today. I have only these three coins.
Reader #5 -	Sighed Chang.

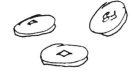

Reader #1 -	Now as Chang walked home, a strange thing happened...
Reader #2 -	Little by little Chang's baskets began to get heavier and heavier.
Reader #4 -	When Chang got home he looked in each basket.
Reader #1 -	Chang could not believe his eyes.
Reader #2 -	Both baskets were filled with coins!
Chang -	What magic! I am now a rich man indeed!
Reader #1 -	Said Chang as more and more coins piled on top of the baskets.
Chang -	I do not need to sell rice any more. I shall help poor people. They can come and borrow money from me.
Reader #5 -	Chang said with a smile.
Reader #4 -	So Chang opened a pawnshop, where poor people could come to borrow money or sell their small treasures.

Reader #2 -	Now at first Chang was both honest and helpful. He helped poor people and was indeed kind.
Reader #3 -	But as Chang earned more and more money, his kind heart changed.
Reader #2 -	Chang became <u>very</u> greedy and cruel.
Reader #1 -	Chang cheated people and took their money. He did not help poor people...
Reader #3 -	He only helped himself.
Chang -	Ah! What a rich man I am!
Reader #4 -	Chang would say each night when he counted his money.
Reader #5 -	Day after day Chang's only thought was to make more and more money.
Reader #4 -	He did not care if he cheated people...he only cared about himself.

Reader #3 -	Now one day an old man **came into** Chang's shop.
Reader #5 -	The old man **wished** to sell **a piece** of jade.
Reader #1 -	The old **man did not** seem to **know** the value **of the jade.** He asked for only three **coins.**
Chang -	What a foolish **old man!** That jade is worth far **more than** three coins.
Reader #4 -	Chang thought **to himself.**
Reader #5 -	So Chang **took the jade** and put it in his pocket. **Then Chang** gave the old man three **coins knowing** that he had cheated **the old** man.
Reader #2 -	No sooner had **the old man** gone when Chang smelled **cloth** burning.
Reader #3 -	The pocket in **which** Chang had placed the jade was smoking!
Reader #4 -	As Chang beat out the fire, the jade fell to the floor.

Reader #5 -   Now the jade was as hot and as red as burning coal.

Reader #1 -   In an instant, the floor was burning...and then the whole shop went up in flames.

Reader #4 -   Chang ran for his life. As he left the burning shop, Chang grabbed the only thing he could.

Reader #3 -   Chang had grabbed the two baskets and the pole...the things he used when he was a poor man selling rice on the streets.

Reader #2 -   Chang opened the baskets. He was sure that all of his money would be inside the baskets.

Reader #1 -   But the baskets were as empty as could be.

Reader #3 -   Then Chang knew who the old man with the jade had been...

Reader #5 -   Can <u>you</u> guess who it was?

Chang -   Why, it was the old man with the
                      tiny rice bowl. He came back to
                      teach me a lesson.

Reader #5 -   Said Chang.

Chang -   Well, at least I have my baskets and
                      stick.

Reader #5 -   Chang said with a sigh.

Reader #4 -   So Chang went back to selling rice
                      on the streets of China.

Reader #1 -   For the rest of his days he carried
                      his baskets and walked through the
                      streets.

Reader #3 -   Chang always looked for the
                      strange old man...the one with the
                      tiny rice bowl and the three coins...

Chang -   But alas, I never saw that old man
                      again.

All -   The End

- Help students locate China on a map or globe. Bring in books to help students get a notion of how people dressed in China long ago. Bring in a rice bowl and gong if you have them. Give your students a rich background about China, its people, its history and folklore. Your students are a captive audience - CAPITALIZE on their interest!

- After reading the script several times, have students discuss the story in small groups. Did Chang learn a lesson? What did Chang learn about money and greed? What is the significance of the three coins?

- There are <u>many</u> excellent books featuring Chinese folktales available...and children <u>LOVE</u> them. Why not set up a center with a wide variety of Chinese folktales?! After reading and sharing them with your students, you may wish to script some of the stories and perform them for other classes.

- Here are a few of my favorites:

  - <u>The Magic Wings</u>
    by Diane Wolkenstein

  - <u>Yeh-shen - A Cinderella Story from China</u>
    retold by Ai-Ling-Louie

  - <u>The Luminous Pearl</u>
    by Betty L. Torre

  - <u>8,000 Stones</u>
    by Diane Wolkenstein

  - <u>Lon Po Po - A Red Riding Hood Story from China</u>
    by Ed Young

Be on top of it all...
READ!

What a Bright idea!

Meet Benjamin Franklin- A Great American

A Reader's Theatre Script
Written and Developed by Lisa Blau

Historian #1   Historian #3   Benjamin Franklin
Historian #2   Historian #4

Benjamin Franklin - Good morning! We're here to tell you all about one of the most famous Americans of all time...

All - Benjamin Franklin!

Historian #2 - Benjamin Franklin was born on January 17, 1706.

Historian #4 - As a young boy, Benjamin enjoyed reading books and writing stories. He taught himself how to do math.

Historian #3 -

He was the youngest son in a family with seventeen children. He only went to school for two years. Then he went to work for his father making candles and soap. When he was twelve he became an apprentice at a printer's shop. He learned how to print books and newspapers.

Historian #2 -

Throughout his life, Benjamin Franklin created many inventions. He invented bifocal eyeglasses so that people could see better. Bifocal lenses help people see greater distances and are also used for reading.

Historian #4 -

Benjamin Franklin invented the Franklin stove. His stove gave more heat than other stoves and used much less fuel.

Benjamin Franklin -

I also helped organized the first library, fire department and hospital. All of these special services were the very first ones established in America.

Historian #3 -

Benjamin Franklin served as deputy postmaster general in 1753. Mail

service improved greatly under his command.

Benjamin Franklin - In 1778, I was appointed special council to France. I helped write the Treaty of Paris, which ended the Revolutionary War.

Historian #4 - Benjamin Franklin was a great statesman. He helped to write the Declaration of Independence.

Historian #1 - Benjamin Franklin had many great ideas for America. He believed that slavery was wrong. He wanted to make America a better place for everyone.

Historian #3 - Benjamin Franklin was one of America's greatest men.

Historian #4 - He was a printer, writer, inventor, scientist, statesman, and dreamer.

Historian #2 - Today we honor Benjamin Franklin in many ways. Franklin's face has been on stamps and coins.

Benjamin Franklin - And on one hundred dollar bills too!

Historian #1 -	There are many statues honoring this special man.
Historian #3 -	Benjamin Franklin loved to read, he enjoyed writing stories, and he was very curious about the world around him.
Benjamin Franklin -	I hope that all of you will imagine new ideas for your world. Read, study hard, and dream!
Historian #1 -	The End

Kristen

- There are many excellent books about Benjamin Franklin that you will want to have on hand to share with your students. One of my personal favorites is <u>Benjamin Franklin, Scientist and Inventor</u> by Eve B. Feldman (1990 Franklin Watts Company). The text is very interesting and the pictures of Franklin are truly exceptional.

  Other excellent resources include:

  - <u>Benjamin Franklin</u>
    by Chris Looby
    Chelsea House Publishers

  - <u>A Picture Book of Benjamin Franklin</u>
    by David A. Adler
    Holiday House, Inc.

  - <u>What's the Big Idea, Ben Franklin?</u>
    by Jean Fritz
    Coward, McCann and Geoghehan, Inc.

  - <u>Benjamin Franklin</u>
    by Cass R. Sandak
    Franklin Watts Co.

  - <u>The Many Lives of Ben Franklin</u>
    by Aliki
    Simon and Schuster

- A wonderful read-aloud story will most certainly be enjoyed by all of your students - <u>Ben and Me</u> by Robert Lawson.

- As a pre-reading activity, ask students to share any information they know about Benjamin Franklin. Student responses could be listed on the board. Add new information to the board after students have performed the script several times. What new information was added?!

- Try to impress upon students what life was like in Franklin's day. We must recognize the importance of having students get a sense of life in different eras and places. Have students make comparisons about life today as opposed to life in 1706. A chart such as the one my students prepared below might be beneficial in helping students gain insight to life in Colonial America. Use your scripts and book titles listed earlier to help students learn more about life in Colonial America.

1706	TODAY
• People used candles to light their homes	• People use electric lights
• People traveled on horses	• People travel in cars
• Children left school to learn a trade - they only went to school for a few years	• Children go to high school and college
• People made their own candles and soap	• We buy these items in a store
• People used fire to cook their food	• We use microwave ovens to cook our food

- Science! Science! Science! No need for a lightning storm and kite for this experiment that proves the existence of electricity in the air! All you'll need are some balloons. After blowing up the balloons, have students rub their balloons against their clothing and then place the balloons near their hair. Have a camera on hand to catch students' faces during this hair-raising experiment.

- Discuss how an electric charge was created. Tell students that as they rubbed the balloon across their clothing, they were actually rubbing electrons from their clothing onto the balloons. The balloon becomes a non-conductor. The electrons no longer flow all around, rather they stay in one place. This is called STATIC ELECTRICITY. The hair acts just like a magnet after becoming positively charged by the balloon.

- Have students write about the results of this experiment in their science journals adding illustrations. Have the entire class help write captions and information to go along with your photographs of the science experiment in progress.

- Write! Write! Write! A mini-book about Benjamin Franklin is included in this unit. Have students share their mini-books with other classes, then display these books in your classroom or school library.

Benjamin Franklin - A Great American

by _____

_____

Benjamin Franklin was born on January 17, 1706.

Benjamin Franklin liked to _____
and _____.

Benjamin Franklin also_____
_____

I think Benjamin Franklin was a great man because

_____.

_____

Comments Page

♥   Please read your book about Benjamin Franklin to your family and friends. Be sure to have them sign your book. Three cheers to you, Super Reader!!!

Name   **Comments**

Happy, Happy Hat Day!

A Reader's Theatre Script
Written and Developed by Lisa Blau

Reader #1	Construction Worker
Reader #2	Navy Officer
Cowboy	Nurse
Football Player	

Reader #1 -   Good morning! Welcome to our presentation called....

All -   Happy, Happy Hat Day!

Reader #2 -   The third week in January has been chosen as the time of year to celebrate Hat Day. And why not....hats are important to all of us.

Cowboy -   That's right. We cowboys wear hats for protection from the sun. It can get mighty hot and dusty out on the cattle range.

Construction Worker - I am a construction worker. I build tall skyscrapers. I wear a hard hat for protection. A construction site can be a dangerous place, so my metal hat helps to keep me from getting injured.

Navy Officer -

I am a Navy Officer. The hat that I wear is part of my uniform. In fact, all members of the armed services wear hats as part of their uniform. Police officers and fire fighters also wear hats.

Nurse -

I am a nurse. My white hat lets people know about my occupation. Each nursing school has a different style hat for the graduating nurses to wear with pride.

Reader #2 - No one knows for sure when people first began to wear hats. The first hats were for protection from the hot sun, rain, or snow.

Reader #1 - We know that people wear hats for three main purposes.

Reader #2 -   People wear hats for protection.

Football Player -   I wear my helmet during the football game for protection. Would you want a 300 pound linebacker coming after you without a helmet? My hat is for protection...BIG time protection!

Reader #1 -   People wear hats for communication.

Nurse -   Like me. My nurse's hat lets patients know that I'm here to help.

Reader #2 -   People wear hats as decoration. Clowns wear silly hats to make people laugh. Kings and queens wear crowns of jewels. People wear hats because they just plain feel good.

Reader #1 -   I just love to wear my Mickey Mouse hat with the extra-big ears that I got at Disneyland! It's so cool! It's awesome! It's me!

Reader #2 -	Over the years hats of many styles, shapes, and sizes have been worn. In the 1400's ladies wore large cone-shaped hats with veils called hennins.
Reader #1 -	And who can forget Abraham Lincoln's famous hat?
Reader #2 -	Though most hats worn long ago have gone out of style, a few styles including a beret and the turban are still worn today.
Reader #1 -	You can learn a lot about other places and other times by looking at the different kinds of hats that people wear. So, hats off to every-one!
Football Player -	Oh no....not me! I'm not taking my helmet off. That 300 pound line-backer is after me again...YIKES!
All -	Happy, Happy Hat Day, everyone!
Football Player -	The End.

- Hat day is traditionally celebrated on the third Friday in January. It is a <u>wonderful</u> way to honor the many kinds of hats worn all over the world. Here are just a few ideas to help you create a memorable day with your students:

- Read and share *A Three Hat Day* by Laura Geringer with your students. It's the story of R. R. Pottle the Third who <u>loves</u> hats. It's a <u>great</u> story to act out or adapt for a Reader's Theatre presentation. The ending is left wide-open for possible sequels...R.R. Pottle the Fourth loved shoes. Students can work together to create all kinds of wild and wonderful adventures about generations of Pottles!

- You can also read and share Martin's Hats by Joan W. Blot. With the change of a hat, Martin becomes an explorer, an engineer, a chef and much, much, more! Have students brainstorm different jobs and occupations that require hats or head coverings as part of the uniform. Then develop students' prediction skills. Ask students to predict what kinds of hats Martin will wear. You could make cut-outs of the various hats named in the story and mount these on the board along with the occupations named in the story. Then, as you read the story, students can match the words and pictures. This is an <u>excellent</u> strategy to use with your Chapter 1 students to help increase their vocabularies.

- Read and share *Hats Hats Hats* by Ann Morris. This wonderful book of photographs will take students all around the world. Students will see how people all over the world wear a wide variety of hats. A visual feast and a social studies and geography lesson all rolled into one fabulous book! Be sure to have students locate each country on a map or globe thereby increasing map skills and interaction with the text.

- To celebrate Hat Day, ask each student to bring in a hat from home along with the accompanying page. (Note: if you have a problem with lice at your school, be <u>very</u> sure that students do not share hats). Children must bring their hats in a paper bag or box so that no one can see it. Set out 5-6 hats at a time, then ask students to read their hat stories. The remainder of the class must match each hat with an owner by listening for clues in each story. Wow! What a fun way to work on descriptive writing and listening skills all in one great lesson!

- As a math extension, graph hats either by color or style. You could have students make the markers for the graph in the shape of a hat.

- Be sure to take <u>lots</u> of photos on Hat Day to add to your classroom memory book or photo display. You may wish to have prizes for the biggest hat, the zaniest hat, the prettiest hat... Say! Why not ask the students to help you think up some categories for prizes prior to Hat Day... it will help get your students on the right track for bringing in a really terrific and different style hat!

Hats off
for
Hats Day!

Happy, Happy Hat Day!

Dear Parents, and Students,

We will be celebrating Hat Day on Friday, January_____. Please bring in <u>any</u> kind of hat on that day. You can bring in a favorite hat or a homemade paper hat... the choice is yours !!! The zanier, the better! You must fill out the page about your hat and bring it in on Friday. One more thing...we want our classmates to try and guess who's hat is who's, so please be sure to put your hat into a paper bag or box.

See you on Hat Day!

_____

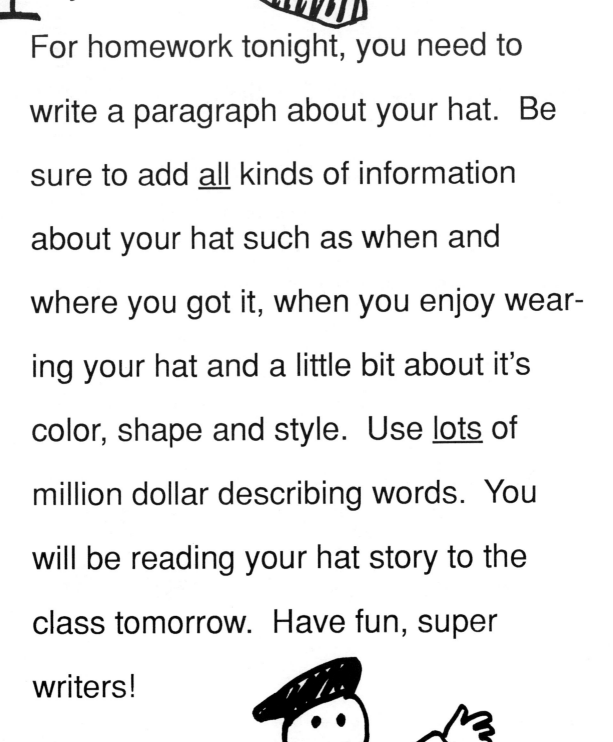

Say Friends!!!

For homework tonight, you need to write a paragraph about your hat. Be sure to add <u>all</u> kinds of information about your hat such as when and where you got it, when you enjoy wearing your hat and a little bit about it's color, shape and style. Use <u>lots</u> of million dollar describing words. You will be reading your hat story to the class tomorrow. Have fun, super writers!

My Hat

by _____

My hat is very special because_____

_____. I got my hat

_____. My hat

is_____,_____

and_____. I enjoy wearing my

hat on_____and_____.

An interesting fact about my hat is_____

_____. My hat is really a terrific one

because_____.

EXTRA! EXTRA! EXTRA! Draw a terrific picture of you and your hat on the back of this paper, Make your illustration bold, bright and beautiful. Have fun, super artists!

Happy, Happy, Happy Hat Day

This certificate is awarded to

_____

for having the

_____

most

hat in

our classroom.

Congratulations and hats

off to you!!!

Love,

_____
teacher's signature

_____
date

place
your
photo
here

Happy Groundhog's Day!

A Reader's Theatre Script
Written and Developed by Lisa Blau

Narrator #1	Groundhog Father
Narrator #2	Groundhog Mother
Narrator #3	Groundhog Pup

Narrator #1 - Good morning! And . . .

All - Happy Groundhog's Day!

Narrator #2 - That's right! February 2nd is Groundhog's Day, so let's find out about this furry little fellow!

Groundhog Father - Well, hello there! I am a groundhog. I'm the only animal that has its own special day on the calendar! That's because people believe that I will wake from my winter's sleep and emerge from my den.

Narrator #3 - Can groundhogs really predict the weather?

Groundhog Mother - Actually, zoologists have studied groundhogs for several decades. They have learned that groundhogs are not very reliable weather forecasters.

Groundhog Father -	The zoologists have learned that most groundhogs are still hibernating throughout February.
Narrator #2 -	Well, I think groundhogs are <u>very</u> cute.
Groundhog Mother -	We have round, furry bodies. We have a flat bushy tail and a stubby nose. We have long whiskers. Our whiskers will help us feel our way around our dark dens beneath the ground.
Narrator #1 -	Groundhogs can be brown, gray, or red. Some groundhogs are pure white with red eyes.
Narrator #3 -	Some people call groundhogs woodchucks. One type of groundhog is called a marmot.
Narrator #2 -	Groundhogs have short legs. Their front paws look like hands. Groundhogs have strong claws for digging.
Groundhog Mother -	We groundhogs like to eat all kinds of plants, fruits, and vegetables. We'll stuff ourselves all summer long with tasty plants. Afterall, we'll be asleep all winter.

Narrator #1 -   A woodchuck has several enemies including foxes, bears, hawks, and owls.

Groundhog Pup -   Squeak! Squeak! I am a baby groundhog. Baby groundhogs are called pups. We are <u>very</u> tiny when we are first born. We weigh about one ounce. We are only four inches long!

Groundhog Mother -   My pups are born without fur. They are also born blind. They are helpless. Their fur will start to grow in two weeks.

Groundhog Pup -   Our eyes will open when we are four weeks old. Our mother will take good care of us. She will teach us what to do if danger is near. We even snuggle and kiss our mothers by touching noses with her.

Groundhog Mother -   I take very good care of my pups. Father groundhog never goes near his babies. I will teach my pups how to dig a den and how to find food.

Groundhog Pup -   As we grow bigger our mother will dig a new den for us.

Groundhog Mother -   Our underground dens have long tunnels, many rooms, and several doorways. There may be a look-out or "spy hole" for us to search for our enemies.

Narrator -

A groundhog will sit up and listen for danger. If a groundhog senses danger, he will send out a shrill whistle. This warning will send the groundhog family deep down under the ground into their dens.

Groundhog Pup -   So, now you've learned all about the furry, famous mammal who has its very own special day on the calendar and . . .

Groundhog Mother -   So we say to you . . .

All -   Happy Groundhog's Day!

Narrator #2 -   The End.

- Prior to reading the script, review new vocabulary words. In an effort to increase my students' vocabulary, I have purposely written the script with several new or more difficult words. You may wish to list the following words on the board to review and discuss at this time:

emerge	forecaster
reliable	colonial
zoologist	predicting
hibernating	

- As a second pre-reading activity, ask students if they know what is special about February 2nd. You may also ask students to tell what they know about groundhogs. A web or cluster would be a perfect way to display student responses. After reading the script, new information can be added to your cluster.

- How well did you listen?! Ask students to answer the following questions about groundhogs:

1. What is another name for groundhogs?

2. What do groundhogs eat?

3. Tell two facts about groundhog babies.

4. Tell three facts about a groundhog's den.

5. Can groundhogs really predict the weather?

Note:

The student responses to these questions can be added to your cluster. You may also wish to have students formulate their own questions for their classmates. Students love playing the part of the teacher. If a student doesn't know an answer, he must read through the script again.

• Read! Read! Read! Here is a list of some of our favorite books about groundhogs. This collection of both fiction and non-fiction books will certainly enhance your study of groundhogs. Place them in a special learning center so that all of your students have a chance to read and enjoy these special books.

- *Woodchuck*
  by Faith Mc Nulty

- *Wonders of Woodchucks*
  by Sigmund A. Lavine

- *About Creatures That Live Underground*
  by Melvin John Uhl

- *Wake Up, Groundhog*
  by Carol L. Cohen

- *What Happened Today, Freddy Groundhog?*
  by Marvin Glass

- *The Happy Day*
  by Ruth Krauss

- *A Garden for Groundhog*
  by Lorna Balian

- *Wake Up, Vladimir*
  by Felicia Bond

- *Will Spring Be Early?*
  by Crockett Johnson

- *Has Winter Come?*
  by Wendy Watson

Be on top of it all... READ!

- Science! Science! Science! A study of shadows and what causes them can be a natural extension to this unit. Use the "Me and My Shadow" worksheet. Your students will also enjoy reading the following shadow books:

  - *Nothing Sticks Like a Shadow*
    by Ann Tompert

  - *The Shadow Book*
    by Beatruce Schenk De Regniers

  - *The Shadow Maker*
    by Ron Hansen

  - *Shadow Magic*
    by Seymour Simon

- The "Me and My Shadow" worksheet is a perfect big-buddy activity for teachers who use upper-grade buddies. Be sure to take photos of this special event. Encourage upper-grade students to share their knowledge of shadows with your students. Upon completion, display the shadow outlines of students, the worksheets, and photos together on a bulletin board. Kids will read the display again and again!

- You can also have students learn about shadows by having them make their very own sundials. This is a really fun lesson because your students will also learn about the concept of time. A sundial can be made from a cardboard box placed on a flat surface. Next cut a hole in the center of the box just big enough to hold a broomstick. Flatten the paper plate and mark the hours in clockwise fashion and insert the broomstick. Have students observe their sundial throughout the day. Students can make illustrations to show how the shadow made by the broomstick changed. Your students can also discuss the accuracy of their sundial.

- As a final science-related activity, your students may wish to learn how other animals survive through the cold winter months. Students can select any number of animals to read about including bears, raccoons, squirrels, and fish. The "Winter Sleepers Worksheet" can be used to help students organize the information about each animal. An excellent way to bring science and language arts together!

Me and My Shadow

A Super Science Worksheet

• You will need a large piece of chart paper for each student, crayons, and a sunny day. Step onto the paper and have a partner trace around your shadow early in the morning. Mark the time next to your outline. Repeat this three times during the day. Be sure to record the time next to each outline. Now answer these questions about your shadows:

1. How did your shadow change?_____
   _____

2. When was your shadow the largest?_____
   _____

3. When was your shadow the smallest? _____
   _____

4. What did you learn about your shadows?_____
   _____

Name_____
Super Scientist

Winter's Sleeper's Record Sheet

Name: _____
My Winter Sleeper _____

Important Facts:
1. _____
2. _____
3. _____

Tell About Your Animal's Home:
1. _____
2. _____
3. _____

Tell About How Your Animal
Prepares for Winter:
1. _____
2. _____
3. _____

Draw your winter sleeper. What does your animal do to prepare for winter? Show this in your picture.

They Called Him Honest Abe

The Story of Abraham Lincoln
A Reader's Theatre Script
Written and Developed by Lisa Blau

Reader #1	Reader #3	Reader #5
Reader #2	Reader #4	Reader #6

Reader #1 -   Abraham Lincoln was the sixteenth President of the United States.

Reader #2 -   He was born on a farm in Kentucky on February 12, 1809.

Reader #3 -   When he was two years old, his family moved to a new farm.

Reader #4 -   Abraham Lincoln helped his father take care of their farm.

Reader #5 -   Abraham Lincoln worked hard planting corn and pumpkin seeds.

Reader #6 -   Abraham Lincoln loved animals. He liked to walk through the woods near his farm. He liked to spend time with the animals.

All -   And they called him, "Honest Abe".

Reader #2 -   Abraham Lincoln always worked hard in school.

Reader #4 -   He had to walk many miles each day to get to his school.

Reader #5 -   Abraham liked school. He loved to read.

Reader #6 -   When Abraham Lincoln was seven years old his family moved to Indiana.

Reader #1 -   Abe helped his father build a log cabin and furniture for their new home.

All -   And they called him, "Honest Abe".

Reader #3 -   As a teenager, Abraham Lincoln read every book that he could find.

Reader #5 -   Once he walked twenty miles to borrow a book.

Reader #6 -   Another time he worked three days for a farmer so that he could pay for a book that got wet in the rain.

Reader #4 -   Abe grew tall and strong. He earned money splitting rails.

Reader #2 -   Abraham always worked hard. He also enjoyed telling stories.

Reader #1 -   Abraham Lincoln was strong, honest, and hard working.

All -   And they called him, "Honest Abe".

Reader #1 -   In 1834, Abraham Lincoln became a legislator for the state of Indiana.

Reader #3 -   He also studied law. He was one of the best lawyers in his state.

Reader #5 -   Abraham Lincoln thought that slavery was very wrong.

Reader #6 -   He made many speeches. He let people know that he wanted to put an end to slavery.

Reader #2 -   In 1860, Abraham Lincoln became President.

Reader #4 -   Abraham Lincoln tried hard to put an end to the Civil War. He wanted all slaves to be free.

Reader #1 -   On April 14, 1865, Abraham Lincoln was shot and killed. Everyone was very, very sad.

Reader #5 -   Americans will always remember Abraham Lincoln for his honesty, goodness, and bravery.

All -   And they called him, "Honest Abe".

Reader #2 -   The End.

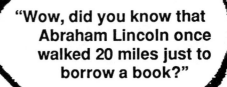

- Be sure to highlight each reader's part for easier reading. You may also wish to review any new vocabulary before students read the script to their classmates.

- The script can be read by any number of students. Encourage students to visit other classrooms to read and share.

- Encourage students to write about facts that they learned after reading and listening to the script. Make a classbook by compiling stories that have been mounted on Lincoln silhouettes.

- Discuss with children the qualities that made Lincoln a great president. What qualities do they admire the most?

- Encourage students to write their own scripts based on the lives of other famous Americans to read and share with others.

- Make a storyline fold-out of Abraham Lincoln's life. Divide a strip of construction paper making a total of 5 parts-then fold. Draw pictures to accompany key events in Lincoln's life. Write a sentence under each illustration. Students can share their work with their classmates.

Kristen

Happy Valentine's Day, Herbie Hartman!

A Reader's Theatre Script
Written and Developed by Lisa Blau

Herbie Hartman	Narrator #1
Mrs. Quarternote, The Music Teacher	Narrator #2
Mr. Fumble, the Coach	Narrator #3
Miss Readsalot, The Librarian	

Narrator #1 -   Welcome and Happy Valentine's Day! We are so glad that you could join us today as we present...

All -   Happy Valentine's Day, Herbie Hartman!

Narrator #2 -   Herbie Hartman is a very special boy indeed. He loves playing football, reading books, and playing his tuba.

Narrator #3 -   Not only that, Herbie <u>loves</u> chocolate and drawing pictures too.

Narrator #1 -	Our pal Herbie is special for another reason...he was born on Valentine's Day.
Herbie - 	That's right! I love Valentine's Day! I love to make cards for all of my special friends. I also love the chocolate candy hearts and kisses that everyone has on Valentine's Day. Man oh man, I just <u>love</u> Valentine's Day!
Narrator #2 -	Every year Herbie makes valentine cards and sends them to all of his friends. He also gives valentines to his Mom, his Dad, and his pet goldfish, Seymour.
Herbie - 	Yep, even Seymour my pet fish loves my valentine cards. How do I know? That cute little rascal swims around and around in his little bowl.
Narrator #1 -	Herbie worked hard making valentines to deliver to his friends the week before Valentine's Day. As Valentine's Day approached, Herbie made his plans...

Herbie -  Aha! I've got it! This year I will give everyone their valentines and as an added treat, I'll throw a party with cake and ice cream and... EVERYTHING! My friends will be so surprised! I can hardly wait!

Narrator #3 -  At last Valentine's Day had arrived. Herbie gathered up all his cards and set out to deliver the valentines to all of his friends.

Herbie - That's when I'll invite everyone to come to my house for the party.

Narrator #2 - Herbie walked down the street and stopped at the first house. He rang the doorbell and waited.

Herbie -  I'm here at Mrs. Quarternote's house. She's my music teacher. I take tuba lessons on Thursdays. Mrs. Quarternote is a great teacher.

Narrator #3 - Just then Mrs. Quarternote opened the door.

Mrs. Quarternote -   Why Herbie Hartman, how nice to see you! But I must tell you Herbie, today is not Thursday. You're here a few days early.

Herbie -   Oh, I'm not here for my tuba lesson. I'm here to give you this valentine. I made it myself.

Mrs. Quarternote -   Why Herbie Hartman, you are so sweet! Thank you so much!

Herbie -   Oh, you're welcome, Mrs. Quarternote. I figure anyone who listens to me play the tuba once a week deserves a valentine card and a few chocolate kisses. By the way, I'm having a Valentine's Day party this afternoon and I sure hope that you can make it.

Mrs. Quarternote -   Oh dear, Herbie. I won't be able to come to your party. Thanks for the card. I'll see you at next week's tuba lesson.

Narrator #2 -   So Herbie said good-bye to Mrs. Quarternote and went to Mr. Fumble's house. Mr. Fumble is

Herbie's football coach. Herbie rang the doorbell and waited.

Herbie -

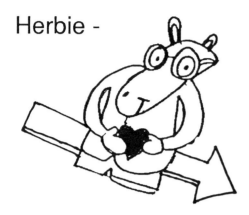

My football coach Mr. Fumble is the best! Even when I ran the wrong way and made a touchdown for the other team, good old Mr. Fumble just smiled and called me, "Wrong Way Hartman."

Mr. Fumble -

Why Herbie Hartman, what a surprise! But our football game isn't until Saturday. You're a few days early, Wrong Way.

Herbie -

Happy Valentine's Day, Mr Fumble. Here's a card that I made just for you.

Mr. Fumble -

Say, isn't that great! I really enjoy getting all those valentines every year from you Herbie.

Herbie -

I'm having a big Valentine's Day party this afternoon. I sure hope that you can come.

Mr. Fumble -

I'm sorry Herbie, but I won't be able to make it today. Maybe next year. I'll see you at our game on Saturday.

Narrator #2 -   So Herbie went on his way to de-liver his next valentine to his friend the librarian. Her name is Miss Readsalot.

Herbie -   Miss Readsalot is terrific! She's always showing me fun new books to read. Her favorite author is Marc Brown. That's my favorite author too! Maybe that's why I like Miss Readsalot so much.

Narrator #1 -   Herbie walked to the library and found Miss Readsalot sitting at her desk reading.

Miss Readsalot -   Why Herbie Hartman! What brings you to the library?

Herbie -   I made this valentine just for you.

Miss Readsalot -   You are such a nice boy! I really enjoy getting your valentines every year. Thank you, Herbie.

Herbie -   You're welcome, Miss Readsalot. And by the way, I'm having a great big Valentine's Day party at my house this afternoon. I sure hope that you can come!

Miss Readsalot -	I'm sorry, Herbie. I won't be able to go to your party. Thanks for the nice valentine. I'll see you when your library books are due next week.
Narrator #3 -	A funny thing happened that day that Herbie just could not explain.
Narrator #1 -	None of Herbie's friends could come to his Valentine's Day party.
Herbie -	I delivered <u>tons</u> of valentines to all my friends, but not a single one can come to my party. I thought it was pretty strange, but I guess I should have invited everyone earlier.
Narrator #2 -	After Herbie delivered his last valentine, he headed for home.
Narrator #1 -	He put the key in the lock and opened the door. And do you know what happened next?!
Narrator #3 -	All of Herbie's friends jumped up and shouted....
All -	Happy Valentine's Day, Herbie Hartman!!!

Herbie -	Wow! What a great surprise!
All -	And happy birthday too!
Herbie -	Gee! Thanks everyone!
Mrs. Quarternote -	Herbie, we wanted to find a way to thank you for all of the terrific valentines that you have given us every year.
Mr. Fumble -	That's right, Herbie. We figured that it was time for us to give you a surprise.
Miss Readsalot -	So here's a big batch of my famous chocolate kiss cookies and a few valentine cards, too.
Herbie -	This has been the best Valentine's Day ever! Let's eat all those treats while I read my valentines.
Narrator #3 -	And that's exactly what they did.
All -	Happy Valentine's Day!
Herbie -	The End.

- This Reader's Theatre script can easily be adapted into a stage play. Have your narrators stand to one side of your stage while the rest of the characters enter and exit the stage as their parts are presented. A painted backdrop of several houses and a library could be designed to enhance your production. If you need more reading parts, just ask your students to write more themselves! Scripting is not only easy, but great fun too! Using sheets of chart paper, students can tell you ideas for additional characters and decide upon each character's speaking parts. Another way to present this script is to simply use two different casts of readers. There are many possibilities here for a fun and memorable way to celebrate Valentine's Day with your class.

- Herbie tells us that both he and Miss Readsalot love author Marc Brown. Be sure to read Brown's super book, Arthur's Valentine. Use the accompanying math page as an extension for this lesson. You will need to fill baggies with a variety of Valentine candies including conversation hearts, chocolate kisses, and red hots (to name a few). Be sure to include some of Hershey's new "Hugs" candies...kids love them!

- The recipe for Miss Readsalot's Valentine Chocolate Kiss Cookies and a few other valentine recipes are included here for you.

Miss Readsalot's Valentine Chocolate Kiss Cookies

1/2 c. margarine	1 egg
1 3/4 c. flour	1 tsp. vanilla
1/2 tsp. baking soda	1 pkg. chocolate kisses
3/4 c. brown sugar	granulated sugar

Directions: Sift dry ingredients. Cream margarine and sugar. Beat in egg and vanilla. Blend in dry ingredients. Shape into small balls, about the size of a teaspoon. Roll in granulated sugar. Bake at 375º for 8 minutes. Remove from oven. Place chocolate kiss in the center of each cookie. Bake 1-2 minutes longer. Yummy!
Note: You can also use your favorite peanut butter cookie recipe too!

Simply Sensational Strawberry Orange Smoothies

1/2 c. sliced and sweetened strawberries
1/2 c. orange juice
3 ice cubes

Directions: Place the ingredients into a blender and blend for 30 seconds. Ah....simply sensational!

Herbie Hartman's Mini Fun Chip Valentine Cookie Bars

2 1/4 c. flour   3/4 c. packed brown sugar
1 tsp. baking soda   1 tsp. vanilla
1 tsp. salt   2 eggs
1 c. softened margarine   1 large package mini fun chips
3/4 c. sugar   colored sprinkles (optional)

Directions: Preheat oven to 375º. In a small bowl, combine flour, baking soda and salt; set aside. In a large bowl, combine margarine, sugar, brown sugar, and vanilla; beat until creamy. Beat in eggs. Gradually add the flour mixture. Stir in the Mini Fun Chips. Spread batter into a greased and floured 15x10 pan. Sprinkle the top with colored sprinkles, if desired. Bake at 375º for 20 minutes. Let cool one hour before cutting into squares...yummy!

Name_____

Arthur's Valentine
by Marc Brown

Directions: Take the candy out of your baggie and sort it according to each kind. Now fill in your graph. When you are all done, you can eat your Valentine treats!

7				
6				
5				
4				
3				
2				
1				

Type of
Candy _____ _____ _____ _____

Super Math Challenge - Write two story problems about your valentine treats on the back of this page. Show all of your work, please!

Now That Winter's Almost Over

A Reader's Theatre Script
Based Upon a Poem by Lisa Blau

Reader #1	Reader #3	Reader #5
Reader #2	Reader #4	

Reader #1 -

Now that winter's almost over,
Now that spring is almost here,
There are a few things that I can
say good-bye to with cheer.

Reader #2 -

Good-bye to dreary grey skies,
Farewell to puddles that never seem
to dry. Good-bye to hats, coats and
snowflurries racing by.

Reader #3 -

Now that winter's almost over,
Now that spring is almost here,
There are a few things that I can
say hello to with cheer.

Reader #4 -   Welcome to April showers,
                     Greetings to fields of wildflowers,
                     Welcome to robin red breast on the
                     wing and to playing baseball for
                     hours.

Reader #5 -   Now that winter's almost over,
                     It's time to dance and sing,
                     Good-bye old man winter
                     I'm so glad it's finally spring!

♥   **<u>A Note For Teachers:</u>**

  Have students use the accompanying poetry worksheet to create their
own poems. Encourage children to use their word lists to help with
ideas and correct spellings. As with tradebooks, using poetry is an
<u>excellent</u> way to help children improve their writing. Don't
forget...children <u>love</u> poetry!

Poetry Worksheet for *Now that Winter's Almost Over*

by _____

Now that winter's almost over,
Now that spring is almost here,
There are a few things
that I can say good-bye to with cheer.

Good-bye to _____ _____ _____
Farewell to _____ _____ _____
Good-bye to _____ _____ _____
and   _____ _____ _____

Now that winter's almost over,
Now that spring is almost here,
There are a few things
that I can say hello to with cheer.

Welcome to   _____ _____ _____
Greetings to _____ _____ _____
Welcome to   _____ _____ _____
and   _____ _____ _____

Now that winter's almost over,
It's time to dance and sing,
Good-bye old man winter
I'm so glad it's finally spring!

READING
ACHIEVEMENT AWARD
Congratulations, Super Reader!

has read and performed a Reader's Theatre Script on

Date:

Signed,

Certificate
of
Achievement

This certifies that_____
has read and performed a Reader's
Theatre Script entitled
_____.
We salute you, SUPER READER!

Congratulations!

Signed, _____

_____
Today's Date

notes

ABOUT *LISA BLAU,* M.A.

WHAT EDUCATORS SAY...

- "Your workshop evaluations were **outstanding**. We want you back. On a scale of 1 to 5, you are a 5 !!"
  -Dr. Arlene Sukraw
  Staff Development Director
  North Platte, Nebraska

- It is my pleasure to "sing the praises" of Lisa Blau. Her practical and motivating strategies and ideas were presented in a manner that both veteran as well as beginning teachers found **inspirational**. We all left with a renewed commitment to enriching our students' lives through fun and educationally appropriate activities.
  -SueAnn Smith
  Director of Special Services
  Vernon Hills, Illinois

- The information that Lisa shared with our teachers was ready to be taken back to the classroom immediately and applied in a meaningful way with students. **I highly recommend** Lisa Blau.
  -Janet Eubank
  Language Arts Teaching Specialist
  Wichita, Kansas

- Lisa is a motivator. Lisa is creative. Lisa likes doing what she does and you know that fact instantly. Lisa loves people, especially kids. Lisa brings out the best in students, and tosses the rest away. Lisa teaches with a passion for learning that soon scorches the very soul of the learner. Lisa, indeed; personifies a "lust for life". If Lisa Blau wants a job, "You would be a fool not to give it to her". She is one of the best, and always gives a whole lot more than she is ever compensated. Lisa brings real joy to learning and to just associating with her. I count Lisa as a trusted and valued associate, and accomplished educator, and a true friend to kids everywhere.
  -R.H. Iannone, Ed.D., Principal
  Covina Elementary School
  Covina, California

EDUCATIONAL BACKGROUND...

Educator-consultant Lisa Blau has an extensive background in the field of education. As a classroom teacher, Mrs. Blau has worked in the Gifted Program and has also served as a Chapter I Resource Specialist. Her wealth of knowledge regarding whole language philosophy and instruction led to a five year position as a Mentor Teacher. While serving in this position, she trained K-6 teachers on the use of literature-based instruction and whole language strategies and methods.

Mrs. Blau currently makes presentations for teachers across the United States and Canada. While combining educational research and theory, Mrs. Blau provides teachers with strategies and ideas that focus on some of today's most pressing issues including assessment and multicultural education. A frequent featured speaker at conferences across the United States, Mrs. Blau has received high marks from her audiences at the following conferences:

- National Science Teachers
- International Reading Association
- California Reading Association
- South-West Regional Self-Esteem
- Washington Reading Association
- Oregon Reading Association
- Idaho Reading Association

She is a recipient of the "Celebrate Literacy" Award given through the IRA for her outstanding contributions to the promotion of literacy.

Mrs. Blau is the author of several Reader's Theatre resource books featuring scripts and extended activities designed to help children discover the joy of reading. An avid reader, Mrs. Blau is happiest when she can read to her children Daniel and Kayla.

STAFF DEVELOPMENT WORKSHOPS by *LISA BLAU*, M.A.
AUTHOR & EDUCATIONAL CONSULTANT

IF YOU'RE LOOKING FOR A DYNAMIC, ENTHUSIASTIC, AND MOTIVATING STAFF DEVELOPMENT CONSULTANT, CALL **800-292-6202** FOR MORE INFORMATION ABOUT *LISA* COMING TO <u>**YOUR**</u> SCHOOL!!!!!

FOR EDUCATORS....

- Learn how to enhance your language arts program through effective research-based strategies and methods.

- Discover how to create a dynamic writing program emphasizing writing as a process.

- Learn how to design a **balanced** curriculum which draws its strength from the best of both phonics-based and literature-based instruction.

- Learn the <u>best</u> strategies to use with Title I students - ideas that can be implemented <u>immediately</u> in any classroom.

- Discover easy ways to incorporate literature into your math program with strategies based upon the NCTM standards.

- Mrs. Blau's presentations emphasize issues such as scheduling, spelling, assessment, and multicultural programs.

- Learn how to use literature, hands-on experiments, and at-home family activities to enhance your science program.

- A <u>Staff Development</u> program specifically designed to meet the needs and interests of your school's teachers can easily be arranged.

- Mrs. Blau's **parent presentations** are an ideal way to help parents gain new ideas to help their children with at-home learning--particularly Title I families.

FOR PARENTS....

- Learn how to share books with your children through exciting family activities such as a *Family Book-nik or Reading Night.*

- Discover countless strategies for helping your child with homework and other school projects...all without tears.

- Learn how to develop your child's interest in writing, science, and math with <u>creative at-home activities</u>.

- Discover the wonderful world of children's books -- what's new in children's literature and what titles are just right for your child's abilities and interests

- Pre-school parents will benefit from Lisa's presentation featuring ideas for helping young children get **hooked on books!**

- Arrange for a BOOK FAIR as a fund raiser for your school or special group as part of Mrs. Blau's presentation.